WOUNDED KNEE

WOUNDED KNEE

Neil Waldman

Atheneum Books for Young Readers

NEW YORK LONDON TORONTO SYDNEY SINGAPORE

A portion of the publisher's profit and the author's royalty is being donated
to the Oglala Lakota College Endowment Fund
Oglala Lakota College
537 Piya Wiconi Road
Kyle, South Dakota 57752

Atheneum Books for Young Readers
An imprint of Simon & Schuster Children's Publishing Division
1230 Avenue of the Americas
New York, New York 10020

Book design by Angela Carlino

The text of this book is set in Bembo.
The illustrations are rendered in acrylic.
Printed in Hong Kong

2   4   6   8   10   9   7   5   3   1

Library of Congress Cataloging-in-Publication Data
Waldman, Neil.
Wounded knee / by Neil Waldman.—1st ed.
p.   cm.
Includes bibliographical references.
Summary: Recounts the events leading to the massacre at Wounded Knee, concluding with a
description of the battle itself.
ISBN 0-689-82559-5
1. Wounded Knee Massacre, S.D., 1890—Juvenile literature.
2. Dakota Indians—Wars, 1890-1891—Juvenile literature. [1. Wounded Knee Massacre, S.D., 1890.
2. Dakota Indians—Wars, 1890-1891. 3. Indians of North America—Wars.] I. Title.
E83.89.W35   2000   973.8'6—dc21   99-020424

FIRST
EDITION

PAGE i: THREE BRAVES FROM A PHOTO BY EDWARD S. CURTIS
PAGE iii: CHE TAN SKA, WHITE HAWK, AN OGLALA WOMAN FROM A PHOTO BY
ALEXANDER GARDNER

MY THANKS TO GEORGE HORSE CAPTURE FOR
HIS CAREFUL READING AND THOUGHTFUL EVALUATION
OF THIS MANUSCRIPT.

———————

To Rex Alan Smith, in recognition of his tireless efforts
to uncover the truth of what really happened at
Wounded Knee. His good works have been my inspiration
and my grist, allowing me to deliver this story to an
audience of young readers for the first time.

CONTENTS

PINE RIDGE RESERVATION CABIN

CHAPTER 1

Massacre

THE SILVER SUN *rose above the hills, sparkling on the frost-coated grasses of Pine Ridge Reservation. Black Elk, a young Lakota warrior, opened the door of his cabin and walked slowly out into the chill morning air. His breath puffed from his lips like small white clouds of smoke as he approached a group of tethered ponies.*

Then, suddenly, a volley of gunfire erupted in the distant hills to the east, and Black Elk froze.

"The sounds went right through my body," he would say later, "and I felt that something terrible would happen."

Black Elk charged back inside the cabin. He quickly found his sacred shirt, with the painting of a spotted eagle spread across the back, and put it on. He hurriedly painted his face red. He wove an eagle feather into his hair. Then Black Elk grabbed his sacred bow, ran out toward the ponies, and galloped off into the hills.

After a short while he was joined by a band of twenty braves, and they rode on together toward the crackling gunshots.

In the distance, they saw a single rider approaching. He was calling out to them as he rode.

BLACK ELK

"Hey-hey-hey!" he yelled. "They have murdered them!" The rider bolted past them, heading back toward the cabins.

The braves galloped onward and soon began hearing terrible shrieks and cries coming from just beyond their sight. They raced to the top of a high ridge, where they looked out into the distance. Before them were scores of blue-coated cavalrymen riding along a steep hillside that paralleled a riverbed. The cavalrymen were shooting their guns downward into it. Just beneath them, groups of women and children zig-zagged frantically in and out of the dwarf pines, struggling to elude the bullets of the bluecoats. Many fell as they ran, their blood flowing into the waters of Wounded Knee Creek.

"Take courage," Black Elk uttered to the braves. "These are our relatives. We will try to get them back."

Then, the twenty warriors began to chant:

> A thunder being nation I am, I have said.
> A thunder being nation I am, I have said.
> You shall live.
> You shall live.
> You shall live.

They charged down from the ridge, directly into the fire of the cavalry. Black Elk held his bow high as he rode. Bullets whizzed past his ears, but none found its mark. He neared the women and children and could see that many were already dead. Some lay piled together for protection, while others were strewn singly alongside the riverbed. A handful were still alive. Two little boys were firing rifles at the bluecoats. An infant was trying to suck milk from the breast of its dead and bloodied mother. Several women and children lay huddled and shivering, barely protected by the slender trunks of the pine trees.

Eventually, the braves were able to drive the cavalry back to their camps.

Later that day, Black Elk walked out along the bloodstained banks of Wounded Knee Creek. He came upon the lifeless bodies of more than one hundred and forty men, women, and children.

"When I saw this I wished I had died too," Black Elk later lamented.

That night, a blizzard descended upon the creek, freezing the broken bodies and burying them beneath a bank of drifting snow.

Thus ended the last battle between two proud and warring peoples. It was the inevitable conclusion of the clash between two disparate nations, the end of the culture of nomadic hunters who had roamed the great plains of North America for centuries.

CHAPTER TWO

First Contacts

THE SEEDS OF the conflict had been sown centuries earlier, when the two peoples lived thousands of miles apart. In those times, a great and mysterious ocean separated them. From the eastern shores of that wild uncharted ocean, an Italian sea captain named Christobal Colón (Christopher Columbus) set sail with three small vessels. He had convinced the king and queen of Spain to sponsor the voyage, attempting to discover a new trade route to the rich lands of the Far East. On October 12, 1492, the ships landed on an island that Columbus called San Salvador. His crew was warmly welcomed by a tribe of friendly natives. Believing that he had arrived in the East Indies, Columbus mistakenly named these people Indians.

After accepting the hospitality of their hosts, the sailors kidnapped ten of these "Indians" and carried them back across the ocean. Upon their arrival in Spain, the Indians were displayed before the king and queen and quickly converted to Christianity. Although one of them died soon after his arrival, the people of Spain rejoiced, for the Indian was now a Christian, and his soul was thus acceptable for entry into a place they called heaven.

With the discovery of the "New World," fleets of ships from Europe began sailing westward across the ocean. The first ships brought soldiers and explorers, but later voyages carried people who hoped to make their homes in the lands that were now called the Americas. For hundreds of years, settlers arrived on the east-ern coast, filling it with cities, towns, villages, and farms. Then they began to march westward, felling the trees of the virgin forests, dirtying the clear waters of the rivers, streams, and lakes,

CHRISTOPHER COLUMBUS, BASED ON A PAINTING BY SEBASTIANO DEL PIOMBO

and pushing the Native American tribes from their ancestral lands.

More than a thousand miles from the settlements of the East, on the great plains of the heartland, seven warrior tribes had been living for many generations. Their lands stretched across places now called the Missouri and North Platte Rivers, The Black Hills of South Dakota, the Bighorn Mountains of Wyoming, and much of the present-day states of North Dakota and Nebraska. The largest of the seven tribes were the Minniconjou, the Brulé, the Hunkpapa, and the Oglala, while the smaller ones were the Blackfeet, the Two Kettle, and the Sans Arc. The people of these seven tribes called themselves the Lakota.

The earliest Europeans to make contact with the Lakota were

explorers and fur traders. They exchanged coffee, sugar, guns, and blankets for the skins of buffalo and beaver. Because each desired the goods that the other possessed, the two coexisted peacefully. Some traders even took Lakota wives and were treated by the Indians with respect. They were able to maintain this trading alliance for many years because the people of the distant eastern cities mistakenly believed that the lands of the Lakota lay within a barren and forbidding wilderness that contained nothing of value.

Then, in the spring of 1841, a small string of covered wagons crossed into Lakota lands. They carried sixty-nine men, women, and children attempting to reach California and Oregon. These were daring people, for they knew that they would face terrible hardships. Furthermore, it had been commonly thought that it would be impossible to cross the entire continent by wagon.

But when word reached the eastern cities that all sixty-nine people

COVERED WAGONS

LAKOTA WARRIORS

had arrived safely, the tiny trickle of wagons became a steady stream. Two years later in 1843, more than a thousand people made the crossing.

The Lakota watched with curiosity from the hills as long lines of covered wagons passed through their lands. In retrospect, it seems strange that it took so many years for the warrior tribes to begin attacking the settlers. For although these strange people never asked the Lakota for permission to cross their lands, they carved a wide brown pathway through the prairies, crushing the grasses, and killing deer and buffalo on their passage.

Then, in 1848, gold was discovered in California, and the stream of settlers became a raging river. In 1850 alone, fifty-five thousand people crossed through the Lakota lands on the broadening brown roadway that was now called the Overland Trail. With them the settlers brought sixty-five thousand cattle that trampled and devoured the prairie grasslands as they passed.

But far more devastating than the destruction of the prairies were the terrible diseases the newcomers carried with them. First came a deadly wave of Asian cholera, then smallpox, and finally measles. Because these sicknesses were new to the Native Americans, they had developed no resistance to them.

The bewildered warriors continued to watch the endless lines of wagons pass through the trampled brown earth of their valleys, while within the tipis their wives, children, parents, brothers, and sisters burned with fever and died.

LAKOTA VILLAGE

CHAPTER THREE

On the Warpath

THE INITIAL ATTEMPTS by the Lakota to stop the flow of wagon trains through their lands were small in scale. Bands of riders charged out onto the brown roadway in a show of force, sometimes, shooting wildly into the air as they circled the wagons just beyond rifle range. Occasionally, when they came upon a very small line of wagons, the warriors attacked the settlers, whom they killed or captured, confiscating their horses, cattle, and possessions.

Stories of "frenzied red heathens" swept through the ranks of settlers, and they loaded their wagons with rifles, pistols, and boxes of cartridges. The newspapers caught wind of the situation, and they began printing sensationalized articles that portrayed the Lakota as inhuman, bloodthirsty savages. As a result, the rift between the two peoples widened. The settlers became so panicked that at the sight of an Indian they would often shoot before they spoke.

As tensions rose, the government in Washington tried repeatedly to defuse the growing conflict by sending representatives to sign treaties with the Lakota. But these attempts were often doomed to failure, for the settlers had virtually no understanding of Native American culture. They didn't realize that, in Lakota society, the chiefs did not possess absolute authority over their warriors. Unlike the European system, where officers commanded and foot soldiers were required to follow orders, the Lakota chiefs could only explain their positions and try to convince their warriors to follow them. As a result, many of the peace treaties signed by the chiefs were never accepted by all of the warriors.

Another problem arose from the European concept of majority rule. The leaders in Washington assumed that if they could obtain the agreement of more than half of the people of a particular tribe, the other tribesmen would be required to comply with the treaty. But this was simply not the way of Lakota society, where each brave was expected to follow his own conscience. The results were disastrous. By the early 1860s, in an atmosphere of frustration and growing distrust, the conflict escalated into a full-blown war.

The first major confrontation occurred just east of the Lakota lands, in Minnesota. A "friendly" tribe lived there. They were the Santee, brothers of the Lakota.

By 1860, the Santee were already settled on reservations. While most of the neighboring tribes had been forced onto the western plains, the Santee remained in their ancestral homeland as the white settlements approached and pushed past them. On their reservations, the Santee lived in brick houses, learned American methods of farming from government teachers, sent their children to American schools, and attended church. The white settlers in Minnesota believed that the Santee had been successfully "civilized." But in reality, the people of the tribes were confused and humiliated. Most of their farms were far from successful. The regular allotment of goods and money that the

LITTLE CROW

government had promised to pay them was often late in arriving. As a result, most of the Santee owed large sums to white creditors, and many of them were almost without food.

On Sunday morning, August 17, 1862, the reservation's Episcopal church was packed with worshipers. When services ended, Little Crow, the Santee chief, warmly conversed with the minister and returned to his brick home for a day of sabbath rest. But a mere twenty-four hours later, Little Crow painted his face, mounted a war pony, and led one of the bloodiest uprisings in the war against the settlers.

WHITE SETTLERS IN THE WESTERN TERRITORIES

The whole affair started when a group of hungry Santee teenagers came upon a nest of unattended eggs on the land of a chicken farmer named Jones. One of the boys told his friends that he wanted to steal the eggs. When a second boy warned against doing so, the first boy called him a coward. The second boy was furious. In order to convince the others of his courage, he bragged that he would kill Jones. Moments later, the silence was shattered by a volley of gunfire. The farmer, his wife, and three others had been shot dead.

When the elders of the tribe learned of the killings, they summoned all the braves, and many expressed fears that the entire tribe would be harshly punished for what the boys had done. In the end, they decided to attack before they were found out.

The Santee planned to strike only the soldiers and their forts. But when they had ridden out into the settlements, years of pent-up frustration over their treatment on the reservation overcame them, and the Santee reverted to their traditional methods of warfare. Galloping through the countryside in small bands, they burned farms and houses, killed all the people they could find, scalped them, and mutilated their bodies. When the violence ended, nearly five hundred settlers were dead. Another five hundred had lost their homes.

The Minnesota massacre left an indelible mark on the settlers. They now believed that the Indians could never be trusted again. Thousands of soldiers were rushed into the area in an attempt to protect the civilians from further violence. But these soldiers were of a new breed. When news of the Santee uprising spread east, masses of angry young men volunteered to go west and "slaughter every savage that they encountered."

As the violence escalated, one of the new army officers committed a vile and repulsive act. A peaceful Oglala chief named Two Face learned that a female settler had been captured by a hostile tribe. He decided to buy her from them and return her safely to her people. On his way back, Two Face was met by another

U.S. ARMY VOLUNTEERS

friendly chief named Black Foot. Together they bought the woman and returned her to one of the soldier forts.

Upon entering the stockade, the woman began sobbing hysterically, moaning about how she had suffered at the hands of her captors. The fort commander immediately ordered Two Face and Black Foot hanged. But these two innocent victims were not hanged in the ordinary manner. Instead of having ropes tied around their necks and being dropped from a platform (which usually resulted in a quick death), the two chiefs were lowered slowly with chains that gradually tightened around their necks. The result was a slow and tortuous death by strangulation.

The surrounding tribes learned of this barbaric act and became so enraged that it was soon unsafe for settlers to travel outside their settlements. Within weeks, the Overland Trail became unpassable. Again the federal government attempted to intercede, trying to stem the rising tide of violence. A treaty was drawn up and signed by a handful of "paper chiefs"—Indians who had been selected by government agents to represent their people. The treaty stated that each Lakota family would receive thirty dollars a year for twenty years. By the terms of the treaty the Lakota also agreed to abide by the laws of the government in Washington and to cease attacking the wagon trains on the Overland Trail. Furthermore, they agreed not to interfere with future roads to be established on their lands.

The government representatives returned to Washington and proclaimed that the paper chiefs spoke for more than ten thousand Lakota. This was a clear majority of the seven tribes, thus making the treaty a legally binding document.

The politicans in Washington soon got to work on the "future roads to be established" clause by beginning the construction of a string of military forts and a second westward trail. They called it the Bozeman Trail, and it skirted the borders of the land that belonged to one of the Lakota tribes, the Oglala. But here, the whites again exhibited their ignorance of Lakota ways, for in the minds of the Oglala the lands just beyond their western borders were actually their own. It didn't matter that they had temporarily lost them in a battle against a

WAR PARTY

neighboring tribe. The Oglala viewed the construction of this new trail as an openly aggressive act by the settlers into their sacred lands.

Oglala resistance began almost immediately. They were led by a charismatic chief named Red Cloud, who was so successful at rallying the Oglala warriors that no settler's wagon could safely set out on the

Bozeman Trail. In the spring of 1866, President Andrew Johnson announced that the trail was completely open, but those who attempted to use it knew that this political statement was untrue. During the month of August, thirty-three settlers met violent deaths along the trail, and by September it was closed. With the Bozeman Trail closed, the Oglala took a short respite, going off on their annual fall hunt. They returned in the early winter to continue their war on the soldier forts that had been built to protect the new trail.

The largest contingent of soldiers was stationed at Fort Phil Kearney in Wyoming, and so the Oglala warriors decided to make their winter camps in the foothills that surrounded the fort. Three hundred soldiers watched nervously from behind the stockades as more than fifteen hundred Lakota warriors gathered in the hills, waiting for the right moment to strike.

That moment came during the daily wood-gathering mission, when a team of soldiers left the fort under armed escort in order to collect firewood for their wood-burning stoves. When a party of Oglala braves attacked the wood gatherers, a rescue force of eighty soldiers charged to the aid of their comrades. They were led

RED CLOUD

by a captain named William Fetterman, a Civil War hero who had recently come to Indian country "to teach the savages a lesson they'd never forget."

Fetterman rushed out into position, determined that he would now get the opportunity he'd been craving. However, the unsuspecting captain was about to be lured into a trap. Fetterman was under orders not to pursue the Indians very far, but he quickly decided to disregard the directives of his commanding officer. It was his intention to force the attacking Oglalas to stand and fight. But each time Fetterman's soldiers charged, the Indians retreated a bit and waited for the next charge. In this way, they drew the soldiers farther and farther from the protection of the fort. Finally, the enraged officer led his soldiers over a hill, where a thousand Lakota warriors lay silently in wait. Fetterman's party was immediately surrounded. Forty minutes later, they were all dead.

In Washington, President Johnson saw that the Indians were winning, so he proposed yet another treaty. In order to convince the Lakota to sign, his envoys offered to abandon the Bozeman Trail.

CHAPTER FOUR

The Shrinking Lands

IT **WAS THE** winter of 1868, and a group of the president's envoys came to Lakota territory carrying suitcases filled with papers. These documents clearly stated that all lands "commencing on the east bank of the Missouri River . . . to a point opposite where the northern line of the State of Nebraska strikes the river . . . and along the northern line of Nebraska . . . shall be set apart for the undisturbed and absolute use and occupation of the Indians. . . . The United States hereby agrees and stipulates that the country north of the North Platte River and east of the summits of the Bighorn Mountains shall be held and considered to be unceded Indian territory, and also stipulates and agrees that no white person or persons shall be permitted to settle . . . without the consent of the Indians."

Furthermore, the treaty went on to reward those Indians who agreed to farm on assigned parcels of reservation land by giving the most successful farmers bonuses and providing each farming family

GOVERNMENT ENVOYS MEETING LAKOTA CHIEFS AT FORT LARAMIE

with "one good American cow, and one good well-broken pair of American oxen . . . seeds and agricultural implements . . . and an allotment of twenty dollars per year." Those who continued to hunt would receive no equipment of any kind and only ten dollars per year. The government would also provide "for males . . . a suit of good substantial woolen clothing . . . and a pair of homemade socks . . . for each female . . . a flannel skirt . . . a pair of woolen hose, twelve yards of calico, and twelve yards of cotton." Each family would also receive "one pound of meat and one pound of flour every day."

BLACKFEET FAMILY, HUSBAND IN "CIVILIZED" CLOTHING

In return, the government in Washington required that the Lakota "will never kill or scalp white men ... [will] relinquish all right to occupy the territory outside their reservation ... and ... compel their children, male and female, between the ages of six and sixteen, to attend school."

After much discussion, most of the Lakota chiefs agreed to put pens to the treaty. For the territory "given" them was almost exactly what they still possessed. Furthermore, the treaty stated that no settlers would be allowed to take any

THE BLACK HILLS

more Lakota lands. The sacred Black Hills, where the Great Spirit dwelled, were nestled safely within their borders.

Still, there were several important chiefs who refused to sign. Among them were Hump of the Minniconjou and Sitting Bull of the Hunkpapa, who stated that they would never put pens to another white man's paper.

The bulk of the Lakota chiefs returned to their people with feelings of satisfaction and hope. After all, they had managed to retain virtually all of their lands, while securing many promises from the whites. Few among them realized it then, but their compliance with this new treaty would soon mean the end of their ancient way of life.

WAITING FOR FOOD AT STANDING ROCK RESERVATION

In the white man's schools, Lakota children were about to learn that their forefathers were primitive and barbaric and that if they were ever to become a civilized people, they must cast aside the ancient ways. At the federal agencies, where the Indians received their monthly allotment of goods, food, and money, they waited for hours in long, slow-moving lines. Adding to the humiliation, "heads of families" were required to collect the rations, forcing men to do the work that only women had done. Their names were called alphabetically, rather than in the order of their importance, so that chiefs, wise men, and elders were dishonored, treated as though they were no more valued than any common member of the tribe. And as they stood there, waiting for the meager amounts of food that would keep them on the edge of starvation, government officials acted as if they were handing out charity, instead of fulfilling their part of a fair bargain.

While these proud people were diminished and humiliated on the reservations, the leaders in Washington encouraged the destruction of the bison, the ancient food source of the Lakota as well as the other Plains tribes. They realized that once these beasts were gone, the Indians would no longer be able to live as nomadic hunters. It was their plan that all the Indians should eventually be forced onto farms, where they would no longer pose a threat to white society. And so the bison were systematically slaughtered. In the end, the great herds, which had once numbered in the millions, were brought to near extinction, and the families of the nomadic hunters began to starve.

LEWIS PLENTY TREATIES,
A BLACKFEET FARMER

GENERAL GEORGE A. CUSTER

Now, with the signing of the treaty, the tidal wave of settlers resumed their westward expansion. They were soon pressing on the borders of the new reservation. Filled with memories of the Minnesota Massacre, they were outraged that the "red savages" should be allotted a territory so vast, particularly when they didn't even farm the land. They fumed when politicians in Washington handed the Indians "free" food and equipment. They demanded that something be done about it . . . and something soon was.

In 1874, a thousand cavalry troops under the command of General George Armstrong Custer crossed into Lakota territory without permission on route to the Black Hills. Government leaders explained that this was simply a fact-finding expedition. The Black Hills were the only remaining lands in the nation that were untouched and uncharted by government surveyors. The soldiers were entering the reservation in order to map these unknown lands. But the truth was far from this. It had long been rumored that there was gold in the Black Hills, and among Custer's men were two miners who "just happened to be on the expedition."

On July 30, the miners discovered a broad seam of gold, and news of their find soon reached the lands beyond the reservation. Within days, newspapers from coast to coast were filled with headlines such as this one from the *Yankton Press and Dakotian:*

PREPARE FOR LIVELY TIMES!
GOLD EXPECTED TO FALL 10 PER CENT!
SPADES AND PICKS RISING.—THE
NATIONAL DEBT TO BE PAID
WHEN CUSTER RETURNS!

With hordes of whites attempting to force their way into Lakota lands, the government dispatched large contingents of soldiers in a desperate attempt to keep them out. The fortune seekers were furious. On September 3, the following editorial appeared in the same *Yankton Press and Dakotian*:

> *This abominable compact (the Treaty of '68) with the marauding bands that regularly make war on the whites in the summer and live on government bounty all winter, is now pleaded as a barrier to the improvement and development of one of the richest and most fertile sections of America. What shall be done with these Indian dogs in our manger? They will not dig the gold or let others do it. . . . They are too lazy and too much like mere animals to cultivate the fertile soil, mine the coal . . . bore petroleum wells, or wash the gold. Having all these things in their hands, they prefer to live as paupers, thieves, and beggars; fighting, torturing, hunting, gorging, yelling, and dancing all night to the beating of old tin kettles . . . if they have to be supported at all, they might far better occupy small*

reservations . . . than to have exclusive control of a tract of country as large as the whole state of Pennsylvania or New York, which they can neither improve or utilize.

Mobs of settlers pushed to break through the wall of soldiers that stood between them and the Black Hills. Small numbers succeeded in doing so, but they were intercepted by bands of Lakota warriors who promptly killed, scalped, and mutilated them. These incidents increased steadily, and soon, amid yet another rising tide of violence, President Ulysses S. Grant decided to act. A team of representatives was rushed to the Lakota lands with a different kind of offer: this time they proposed to buy the Black Hills from the Indians.

The Lakota rejected their offer, and the whites were incensed. What followed was a series of angry threats and exchanges, resulting in a decision in Washington to send additional troops into the area. Sitting Bull learned of the advancing soldiers, and he dispatched messengers to all the tribes of the Lakota, beseeching them to "come out for one more big fight with the soldiers." Several days later, more than a thousand warriors had gathered, and Crazy Horse led the Lakota against the bluecoats. After several hours of fierce fighting, the soldiers of General George Crook turned and retreated. That night, the tribes camped in the valley of the Little Big-Horn River and held a great war dance, celebrating the events of the day.

On the following morning, June 25, 1876, the Lakota camps were discovered by the soldiers of the seventh cavalry. They were commanded by the now-famous Indian hater, General George Armstrong Custer. A battle ensued, and it lasted a full day. When the sun set, two hundred and sixty soldiers—the entire seventh cavalry—had been killed. Among them lay the body of their famous commander.

CUSTER'S LAST STAND, BASED ON A PAINTING BY CASILLY ADAMS

Aware of the enormity of their victory and fearful of reprisals, the Indians scattered, returning quickly to their reservations. Congress acted swiftly. Another group of officials was sent among the Lakota with a strongly worded proposal: If the Indians continued to refuse to sell the Black Hills, the white government would cease providing them with food and clothing.

PRESIDENT ULYSSES S. GRANT

The chiefs looked out among their pathetic, impoverished people and realized that they had no choice. It was either relinquish the Black Hills or die of starvation. And so, they sadly agreed to sell their most treasured lands.

For several years, the Indians subsisted on the food, money, and clothing that the government provided them by treaty. But then, by an act of Congress, the quantity of provisions was cut nearly in half. In the frozen nights of winter, the starving people were attacked by wave after wave of European diseases, and they began to die in large numbers. But as devastating as all the diseases and physical hardships they had endured was the painful knowledge that their ancient, cherished way of life had died.

CHAPTER FIVE

The Messiah

THE SPIRIT WORLD had always been at the center of the Lakota universe. The Lakota spent their lives in quest of visions that brought understanding and direction. In times of trouble and confusion, they reached into this world, striving the find the sacred power within them.

Such a vision came to a Northern Paiute named Wovoka, who lived in the distant western lands of snowcapped mountains, near the waters of Lake Tahoe. Wovoka had been cutting wood in the mountains when the Great Spirit came to him in a vision. Together, they traveled to the land of the spirits. It was a wondrous place, the most beautiful that Wovoka had ever seen. All the streams were filled with fish, and all the bison that had ever roamed the Great Plains were there as well. Living among the animals were all the Indians who had ever died, alive once again in a new land. The Great Spirit explained that Wovoka was the Wanekia, the Son of the Great Spirit, and he would be

WOVOKA

returned to earth to teach the Indians how to reach this wondrous place. The whites, who had crucified the Wanekia the last time he came to earth, would not be permitted to enter. This time, he was coming for the Indians.

News of Wovoka's vision spread through the destitute reservations, bringing hope to the downtrodden people. Before long, these stories reached over the snowcapped peaks of the Rockies, across the wide grasslands, and beyond the Bighorn Mountains, to the lands of the Lakota. And so it was decided that a party of Lakota representatives would travel west by train to meet and speak with Wovoka. They returned with detailed instructions of what they must do to enter the spirit world.

First, the people were to prepare a log of cottonwood by stripping off most of its branches, painting it red, and decorating it with eagle feathers and strings of many colors. The log was to stand in the center of a large, flat dancing place. Once this was done, the people were to fast for a full day and go to the sweat lodges, where they would be purified. Their faces would then be painted by holy men, and eagle feathers would be threaded into their hair. After donning their sacred shirts and dresses, they would be ready to begin the ceremony, which came to be known as the Ghost Dance. The people would stand in a great circle, holding hands, and begin to chant and dance. The dancing would last for hours. Occasionally, the dancers would fall exhausted onto the ground, and it was then that the visions would come. An Oglala chief named Little Wound later spoke of his experience:

"When I fell in the trance a great and grand eagle came and carried me over a great hill, where there was a village such as we used to have before the whites came into this country. The tipis were all of buffalo skin . . . and there was nothing in that land that the white men had made."

Indeed, many told stories of the wondrous land they had visited, and the Lakota became convinced that they would all soon live there.

But a white reservation official was frightened by the dancing. He wired Washington: "The agency is at the mercy of these crazy dancers.... I deem the situation at this agency very critical, and believe that an outbreak may occur at any time, and it does not seem to me to be safe to longer withhold troops."

In actuality, the settlers were in absolutely no danger. The basic tenets of the Ghost Dancing religion were steeped in the most peaceful of Christian traditions. Wovoka, whom the Indians believed to be the Son of God, preached a doctrine of love and nonviolence. "You must not fight," he had commanded. "You must not hurt anybody or do harm to anyone ... and [you must] live in peace with the whites."

Nonetheless, the dancing terrified the settlers. When the telegram reached Washington, the War Department issued instructions to make ready for the imminent uprising of the Lakota.

Several weeks later, the same frightened official sent another telegraph. "Indians are dancing in the snow and are wild and crazy. I have fully informed you that the employees and government property at this agency have no protection and are at the mercy of the Ghost Dancers.... We need protection and we need it now ... nothing short of 1000 troops will stop the dancing."

Shortly after his message was received, a contingent of cavalry was dispatched to the reservation. It would be their charge to prevent the Lakota from dancing.

Meanwhile, Sitting Bull, chief of the Hunkpapa, became interested in the Ghost Dance. And so he arranged for Chief Kicking Bear, prophet of Wovoka, to come to his home in order to introduce his tribe to the new religion.

"My brothers," Kicking Bear began, "I bring you the promise of a day in which there will be no white man to lay his hand on the bridle of the Indian's horse; when the red men of the prairie will rule the world. . . .

KICKING BEAR

"I bring you words from your fathers the ghosts, that are now marching to join you. They are led by the Messiah who came once to live on earth with the white men, but who was cast out and killed by them. . . . Go then, my children, and tell these things to all the people, and make all ready for the coming of the ghosts. . . . And while my children are dancing and making ready to join the ghosts, they shall have no fear of the white man."

So powerful and convincing were Kicking Bear's words that by the time he finished speaking, all the Hunkpapa had been transfixed by his vision. They were ready to dance. But once all the preparations were made and the Hunkpapa began moving in a great circle, the white agent dispatched a group of Indian policemen to arrest Kicking Bear and escort him back to his reservation.

On the following day the Hunkpapa were dancing once again. And leading them was Chief Sitting Bull. When the white agent learned of

SITTING BULL

the situation, he decided that the great chief must go. "I would respect-
fully recommend," he wrote to the commissioner of Indian affairs in
Washington, "the removal from the reservation and confinement in
some prison . . . of Sitting Bull."

The agent's letter was passed on to the press, and a campaign of wildly exaggerated articles began to appear in newspapers across the country. The *Chicago Daily Tribune* printed the agent's letter under the headline:

To Wipe out the Whites
Old Sitting Bull stirring up the
Excited Redskins

On the same day, this article appeared in the *Chicago Daily Tribune*:

Soldiers Are Ready for Him
The Army in the Northwest Prepared to Quell
Any Uprising

Standing Rock Agency, ND, Oct 27—Special—For the last four weeks Sitting Bull has been inviting the Sioux Indians in this vicinity to an uprising. He enlisted the sympathy of a large number of young bucks by telling them the story of his great bravery on the field of the Custer massacre, and several hundred of them have agreed to go on the warpath.

Actually, while these articles stirred up feelings of fear, anger, and panic among the white settlers, the Hunkpapa continued dancing peacefully. They soon became aware of the wrath of the whites, but they remained unaffected and unafraid, for they believed that their sacred shirts would protect them from any bullets that were fired at them.

Wild rumors began to circulate among the whites. In the town of Mandan, North, Dakota, just outside the Hunkpapa reservation, the people panicked. A sensationalized article in the *Chicago Daily Tribune* was the cause:

Mandan, ND, Nov 16—Settlers on the farms and ranches south of Mandan are fleeing their homes, believing that an Indian uprising in North Dakotah is at hand. They urgently demand protection and many a farmhouse in North Dakotah will soon be deserted unless the settlers receive some assurance that they will not be left to the mercy of the murderous redskins, who are now whetting their knives in anticipation of the moment when they begin their bloody work. The Indians are trading their horses and all other property for guns and ammunition. . . . Joseph Buckley rode in today from the reservation and says . . . every Indian on the reservation will shortly go on the warpath.

On the following morning, a wildly exaggerated tale swept through the settlements like a windblown prairie fire that a band of heavily armed Hunkpapa warriors had just left their reservation. They were already headed for Mandan, bent on killing all the whites and burning the town. The county sheriff immediately wired the federal marshall's office in Fargo: "The Indians are crazy and likely to go on the warpath at any minute. Have telegraphed Governor Miller for arms."

That same day, the *Chicago Daily Tribune* carried an article that read: "It is reported that the Indian police have torn off their badges and revolted. . . . Roving bands that are travelling through the country say that the war of the Messiah will begin shortly, then every white man will be killed."

The terrified people of Mandan bolted to the train station, where the women and children were transported to safety in the city of Bismarck.

In Washington, the Secretary of the Interior placed General Nelson

Miles in charge of restoring peace in the area. Miles, believing that Sitting Bull was responsible for the unrest and that the chief was planning a massive uprising of all the Lakota tribes against the whites, decided to have him arrested. Remembering that William Cody (the legendary Buffalo Bill) was a longtime friend of the chief, and that the two had traveled together in Cody's Wild West Show, Miles sought Cody's help. Cody's reply was swift. He would be glad to approach Sitting Bull. Furthermore, it was his belief that with a bit of persuasion, he would be able to arrange for the chief's peaceful surrender. General Miles then sent Cody the following memo:

CONFIDENTIAL
Headquarters, Division of the Missouri
Chicago, Ill., Nov. 24, 1890
Col. Cody,

You are hereby authorized to secure the person of Sitting Bull and deliver him to the nearest com'g officer of U.S. Troops, taking a receipt and reporting your action.

Nelson A. Miles, Major General, Comd. Division

Upon receiving this directive, Cody packed several leather suitcases with his finest clothes and boarded a train heading for Indian country. En route, he stopped in Wisconsin to pick up some of his old cohorts. They arrived in Bismarck, North Dakota, and embarked on a wild shopping spree. Cody spent hundreds of dollars on a wide array of gifts for his old friend Sitting Bull, including tremendous quantities of candy for the chief's legendary sweet tooth. He then chartered a special train to Mandan, and after a crowd of newspaper reporters climbed on board, they were on their way.

On the following morning, Cody strode into Fort Yates, just across the road from the border of Standing Rock Reservation. Wearing a tailored suit from his Wild West Show, silk stockings, and patent leather shoes, and followed by a colorful entourage of friends and reporters, Cody's grand entrance shocked the agency's commanders. These

COLONEL WILLIAM "BUFFALO BILL" CODY

military men were immediately suspicious of the entire expedition. And so they quickly decided to sabotage it.

While Cody and his comrades were introduced to the fort's officers and offered a drink, Indian agent James McLaughlin quickly dashed off an urgent telegram to Washington:

To Commissioner Indian Affairs:

William F. Cody—Buffalo Bill—has arrived here with a commission from General Miles to arrest Sitting Bull. Such a step at present would be unnecessary and unwise, as it will precipitate a fight which can be averted. A few Indians still dancing, but it does not mean mischief at present. I have matters

well in hand, and when proper time arrives can arrest Sitting
Bull by Indian police without bloodshed. . . . Request Gen.
Miles's order to Cody be rescinded and request immediate
answer.

> *McLaughlin, Agent*

After a night of drink and merriment, Bill Cody's party finally left the fort. Before he boarded one of the wagons the next morning, he turned to the reporters and spoke grandly. "I am off," he proclaimed, "on the most dangerous assignment of my whole career."

They crossed the road, entering the reservation. As they traveled slowly southward, McLaughlin's telegram made its way from the commissioner to two of the president's cabinet members, and finally to the president himself. Meanwhile, back on the reservation, one of the agents intercepted the wagons. The agent told Cody that he had just seen Sitting Bull, who he claimed was traveling northward toward the fort. Cody ordered that his wagons be turned around, and they headed back toward Fort Yates. When they arrived several hours later, McLaughlin handed Cody a telegram:

> *Colonel William F. Cody, Fort Yates, N. D.*
>
> *The order for the detention of Sitting Bull has been rescinded.*
> *You are hereby order to return to Chicago and report to General*
> *Miles.*
>
> *Benjamin Harrison, President*

Cody was furious. He stomped back toward his wagons and led his entourage back to Mandan, where he boarded a train to Chicago.

CHAPTER SIX

Big Foot

AS THE WINDS of winter whistled through the cabins of the reservations, it was decided that Sitting Bull would lead a great gathering of his people in the Ghost Dance. The ceremony was to be held atop a plateau at Pine Ridge, south of Standing Rock Reservation. And so Sitting Bull, in order to inform agent James McLaughlin of his intentions and ask for permission to leave the reservation, had a letter delivered to Fort Yates:

To the Major In Indian Office

I want to write a few lines today to let you know something. I have had a meeting with my Indians today, and I am writing to tell you our thoughts.

God made both the White race and the Red race, and gave them minds and hearts to both. Then the white race gained a high place over the Indians. However, today our Father is helping us Indians—that is what we believe.

And so I think this way. I wish no one to come with guns or knives to interfere with my prayers. All we are doing is praying for life and to learn how to do good. . . .

When you visited my camp you gave me good words about our prayers, but then you took your good words back again. And so I will let you know something. I got to go to [Pine Ridge] Agency and know this Pray [do the Ghost Dance]; so I let you know that . . . I want answer back soon.

Sitting Bull

Agent McLaughlin quickly decided to notify his Indian policemen that Sitting Bull was not to be allowed to leave Standing Rock, ordering them to arrest the chief. These policemen were known to the people of the tribe as Metal Breasts, for the shiny badges they wore. Sitting Bull's followers were quite disdainful of them, for they had chosen the white man's ways. They had become farmers, and received good salaries and fancy uniforms from the government. Most of the people, however, held on to the dream that Sitting Bull would lead them back to

INDIAN POLICEMAN

their cherished ancient way of life. And so, against the government's decrees, they would continue to dance.

On December 15, 1890, in the darkness of early morning, a band of forty-three Indian policemen assembled and rode to Sitting Bull's cabinet. They knocked on the door and found the chief lying naked beneath his winter blankets.

"We come to take you to the agency," they informed him. "You are under arrest."

"All right," Sitting Bull answered. "Let me put on my clothes and I'll go with you." But when the old chief began speaking angrily, and taking longer than the nervous policemen demanded, they hurriedly dressed him. Grabbing both his arms, and with a gun to Sitting Bull's back, they walked stiffly out into the morning.

When they emerged from the cabin, the policemen discovered that they were surrounded by an angry crowd of Ghost Dancers. The policemen attempted to push Sitting Bull toward his horse, but the chief refused to move. "Sitting Bull was not afraid," one of the policemen later commented. "It was we who were afraid."

The Ghost Dancers began pushing the policemen back toward the cabin when the chief's seventeen-year-old son, Crow Foot, called out, "You have always called yourself a brave chief, but now you are letting yourself be taken away!"

"All right," Sitting Bull replied. "I will not go another step!"

Several braves pointed their rifles at the frightened policemen. "Kill them!" someone shouted. "Kill them!" Just then, a shot rang out, and one of the policemen dropped to the ground. As he fell, he pulled the trigger of his pistol, shooting Sitting Bull in the chest. As the chief doubled over another policeman shot at his head, killing him instantly. Just then, as if on cue, Sitting Bull's old show horse sat back on his haunches and raised one of his forehooves. The Indians all froze momentarily, as if they'd seen a ghost. But then the horse sauntered away, and the combatants turned to each other once again.

The frenzied mob charged wildly at the policemen, wielding guns and clubs. The policemen retreated into Sitting Bull's cabin, and they would probably all have been slaughtered had the army not arrived to save them.

Later that day, Hunkpapa warriors and their families began sneaking away from Standing Rock Reservation. Singly and in small groups they traveled south, hoping to find refuge with their brothers, the Minniconjou.

After trekking a hundred miles in four days, a foot-weary Hunkpapa band came upon Big Foot's Minniconjou at Cherry Creek. These Minniconjou had also been traveling for many days, attempting to elude a company of advancing soldiers. They were on their way to Pine Ridge Reservation, where Red Cloud, last of the great chiefs, was still leading his tribe in the Ghost Dance. It was Big Foot's hope that Red Cloud would provide safety and shelter for his people.

The Minniconjou chief had been stricken by pneumonia, one of the white man's terrible diseases. As he led his people on an elusive, winding path toward Pine Ridge, he began to weaken. Several days later, when they were within a long day's walk of their destination, Big Foot began to vomit blood, and he was placed inside a wagon. He lay there shivering beneath a pile of blankets when two of his scouts informed him that the soldiers were camped just ahead of them, at Wounded Knee. A council was called, and many of the braves voiced the opinion that they should turn south and travel in a great circle around the soldiers. But Big Foot was afraid that if they took this longer route, he might die before reaching Red Cloud. And so it was decided that the group would continue onward.

At two o'clock in the afternoon, on December 28, 1890, the bedraggled band of three hundred and fifty Minniconjou and Hunkpapa

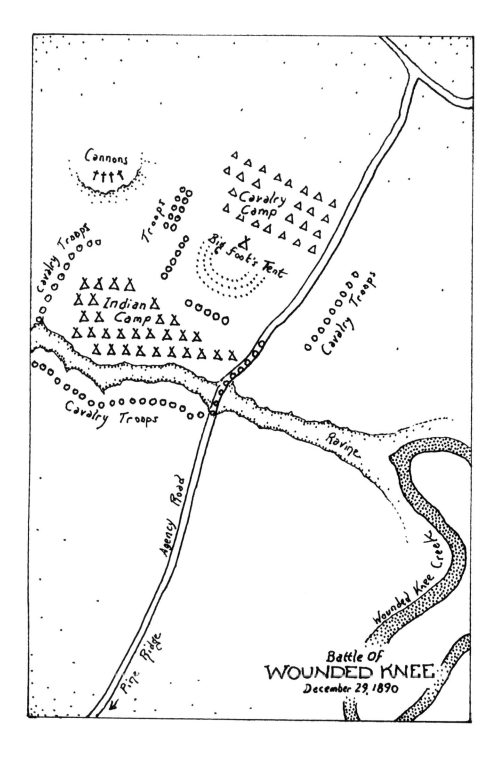

men, women, and children climbed over a ridge and were discovered by the soldiers of Major Samuel Whitside. The soldiers immediately surrounded the Indians and escorted them down the sloping hill to a steep-sided ravine on the banks of Wounded Knee Creek. Whitside ordered the Indians to set up camp there, erecting large tents for those who had no shelter of their own and a separate tent, complete with a wood-burning stove and a doctor, for the ailing Chief Big Foot. Bacon and hardtack (military biscuits), were then passed out, and the famished tribesmen filled their stomachs for the first time in days.

After the sun set, Whitside's troops were joined by the commander of the seventh cavalry, Colonel James W. Forsyth, leading two hundred additional reinforcements. With him, Forsyth carried commands from General Miles that read: "Disarm the Indians. Take every precaution to prevent their escape. If they choose to fight, destroy them."

Now in charge, Forsyth directed his troops to encircle the Indian camp, pointing the long barrels of four small rapid-firing cannons toward the tents and tipis of the sleeping prisoners. After all their soldiers had been deployed and positioned, the officers raised glasses of whiskey, toasting the peaceful surrender of Big Foot.

In the early hours of the next morning, December 29, 1890, Forsyth ordered all Indian males to assemble in front of Big Foot's tent. They sat in a large semicircle as the colonel addressed them. He assured the braves that they had nothing to fear, for their families were safe now. Their rations would be increased so that they would no longer live in hunger. Finally, he explained that before they broke camp, the Indians would be required to give up all their weapons.

At this last command the Indians began stirring uneasily. For even though these bluecoats had treated them well during the past two days, they were white men and not to be trusted. And so the Indians decided

WICAI WE, BLOODY MOUTH, A HUNKPAPA BRAVE

to turn in two old rifles but keep the rest of their weapons hidden. It was then that Forsyth ordered his troops to search the Indian camp.

Within minutes the entire site was bustling with soldiers who unloaded Indian wagons and spilled their meager possessions onto the ground. They tore open the rolled-up teepees, slashed through skin bags, and confiscated any object that vaguely resembled a weapon. As the earth was littered with their belongings, the braves glanced nervously at one another, sensing that a bloody confrontation loomed just ahead.

The soldiers now turned to the women. And as the searchers discovered rifles hidden beneath their skirts and blankets, the men began to stir. Big Foot, lying in front of his tent, asked two braves to lift him, and he attempted to calm his people. But the chief was now so weak that his voice was barely more than a whisper, and the tensions continued to grow. A medicine man named Yellow Bird turned to the young men and yelled, "Look out! Something bad is going to happen!" He then uttered a traditional battle cry that Lakota warriors had chanted for generations:

"I have lived long enough!"

Forsyth ordered that Yellow Bird sit down, and the medicine man complied for a while. But several minutes later he was up and chanting again, as the young braves were brought before the searchers. Two had their guns taken from them. A young warrior jumped up, pulled a rifle from beneath his blankets, and began furiously waving it above his head.

"This weapon is mine!" he shouted. "I paid good money for it, and I will not give it up without being paid for it!"

Another young warrior named Black Coyote tore open a brown paper bag, revealing his rifle. Two soldiers lunged at him, and as they

SLAUGHTER AT WOUNDED KNEE

struggled to take his weapon a gunshot exploded in the air. Within seconds both sides opened fire. As rapid-firing cannons roared, Big Foot struggled to raise himself from the ground. A bullet pierced his skull. Everywhere, wagons and teepees were torn to shreds. Men's, women's, and children's bodies were blown open as they fell to the ground.

Those Indians who survived the first onslaught ran from the camp-site, westward along the ravine. They were mostly women and children, zigzagging frantically between the dwarf pines, attempting to elude the unrelenting hail of bullets. Scores of soldiers charged after them on horseback, their long rifles exploding again as they rode.

BIG FOOT'S FROZEN BODY AT WOUNDED KNEE BATTLEFIELD

Just then, Black Elk appeared on the crest of the hill, along with twenty Lakota horsemen. Their faces were painted bright red. They wore eagle feathers in their glistening black hair. Their sacred shirts fluttered in the wind. The riders held their bows high above their heads and charged down from the ridge, directly into the fire of the cavalry. Their ghostlike chanting echoed through the ravine as they rode:

> A thunder being nation I am I have said.
> A thunder being nation I am I have said.
> You shall live.
> You shall live.
> You shall live.

A short time later, the cavalry retreated to their camps. Black Elk returned to Wounded Knee Creek and dismounted. He felt a wisp of wind pass through him as he walked among the frozen bodies, while in the eerie stillness the blood of the last free Lakotas trickled into the earth.

The battle had ended: the final battle. In the annals of history it would be recorded that on the twenty-ninth day of December, 1890, at Wounded Knee Creek, South Dakota, the last confrontation between two warring peoples had culminated in a white victory.

Years later, Black Elk remarked in words that were recorded in 1932:

"I did not know then how much was ended. When I look back now from this high hill of my old age, I can still see the butchered women and children lying heaped and scattered all along the crooked gulch as plain as when I saw them with eyes still young. And I can see that something else died there in the bloody mud, and was buried in the blizzard. A people's dream died there."

BLACK ELK, A LAKOTA HOLY MAN, IN 1947

Epilogue

ALTHOUGH IT WAS predicted by some whites that Indians would disappear completely, the Lakota and their culture are very much alive. After years of struggle with the Bureau of Indian Affairs and the United States government, they are now working to shape their own destinies. The Lakota today have their own system of education in schools and a tribal college. They are providing social services to their people and they are bringing back the traditions of their ancestors, including the sun dance ceremonies, which were outlawed for many years by the federal government.

The Lakota have been in a struggle with the federal government over their claim to the Black Hills, since they were appropriated by the United States in 1870. Finally, in 1980, they were awarded 106 million dollars in compensation, but the Black Hills Sioux Nation Council refused to accept the money, and demanded the return of the land. Legislation to return the Black Hills to the Sioux has twice been defeated in Congress, but the Lakotas continue to fight.

Looking toward the future, Gene Thin Elk, a professor of education at the University of South Dakota, has said, "We have to have a redefinition of ourselves as individual people and a redefinition of Lakota culture. . . . We can come to the point where we say that poverty is no longer a concept in our existence, that people don't have the power to make us second-class citizens, that we deserve the best the world has to offer, that we are not better than anybody, but that we have an equal right to the universe."

Bibliography

Bordewich, Fergus M. *Killing the White Man's Indian: The Reinventing of Native Americans at the End of the Twentieth Century.* New York: Doubleday, 1996.

Brown, Dee. *Bury My Heart at Wounded Knee.* New York: Henry Holt & Co., 1970.

Neihardt, John G. *Black Elk Speaks.* Nebraska: University of Nebraska Press, 1979.

Rachlis, Eugene. *Indians of the Plains.* New York: American Heritage Publishing Co., 1960.

Schusky, Ernest L. *The Forgotten Sioux.* Chicago: Nelson-Hall, 1975.

Smith, Rex Alan. *Moon of Popping Trees.* New York: Reader's Digest Press, 1975.

Photo Credits

Many of the illustrations in this book are based on early photographs. Most of them can be found at the Smithsonian Institution or the Library of Congress.

The illustrations were based on photographs by Edward S. Curtis (pp. 7, 15), A. Zeno Shindler (p. 10), Alexander Gardner (pp. 19, 46), Rose Tatsey (p. 21), Peter Red Horn (p. 23), David F. Barry (p. 33), and Thomas Magee (p. 41).

Index